*For Oliver, Toby, Rosie and all
the kind people of Huddersgate
without whose help and advice
this book would not have been
possible.*

By the same author
Stanley Bagshaw and the Twenty Two Ton Whale
Stanley Bagshaw and the Mafeking Square Cheese Robbery
Stanley Bagshaw and the Short-Sighted Football Trainer

First published in Great Britain 1981 by
Hamish Hamilton Children's Books
27 Wrights Lane, London W8 5TZ

Reprinted 1983, 1986

Copyright © 1981 by Bob Wilson
British Library Cataloguing in Publication Data
Wilson, Bob
Stanley Bagshaw
I. Title
823'.914[J]   PZ7
ISBN 0-241-10634-6
Printed in Great Britain by
by Cambus Litho, East Kilbride

Stanley Bagshaw

AND THE FOURTEEN-FOOT WHEEL

By Bob Wilsons

Hamish Hamilton · London

In Huddersgate – (famed for its tramlines) up north where it's boring and slow

Stanley Bagshaw resides with his Grandma at number 4 Prince Albert Row

Now, near where Stan lives is a factory
which he frequently happens to pass
that makes sprockets and wheels
out of copper and steel,
and motorbike parts out of brass.

One day Stanley Bagshaw was walking
along by the factory gates
when the works engineer said –

Stanley! Come here.
Will you give me a hand, me old mate?

Good lad.

Yes.

Stanley, being kind and obliging,
said he could spare a moment or two.
So George then began
to explain to our Stan
what he wanted the young lad to do.

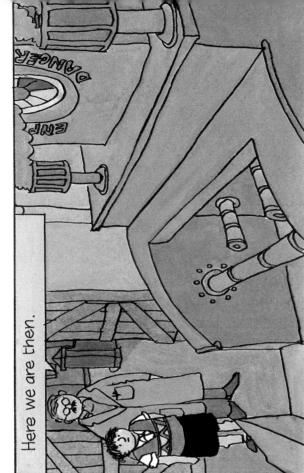

Here we are then.

The tea-lady's off with the measles.
And my tea-break is long overdue.
Will you keep an eye on the foundry
while I put on the pot for a brew?

I bet she's spotty.

That's a mould-grommet.

Oh yes.

That's the sprocketogriffier.

I see.

You see that big clock in the middle? That shows when the wheel-mould is full. Now, here's what you do. When it says thirty-two, you just give this big lever a pull.

EMPTY
FULL
DANGER
32

Now I'll only be gone for a moment so don't worry - [the engineer said] Are you sure that you understand what to do?

Our Stanley just nodded his head.

He fell so fast asleep that he snored.

Well, at first the job seemed quite exciting but Stan soon got so tired and bored

he just couldn't keep from falling asleep.

But the hands on the clock kept on turning –
thirty-two... thirty-three... thirty-four...

Past the red danger sign – thirty-eight... thirty-nine
till the mould wouldn't hold anymore!

Our Stanley just nodded his head.

By gummy!
[the engineer said]
Stanley Bagshaw have you
let it pass thirty-two?

Just look at that clock!
[shouted Cyril]

Then George gave a pull on the lever.
The machine gave a strange clunking sound.
Then . . . . . what a surprise!

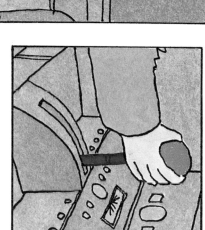

Just look at the size! [shouted George]
It's near fourteen foot round.

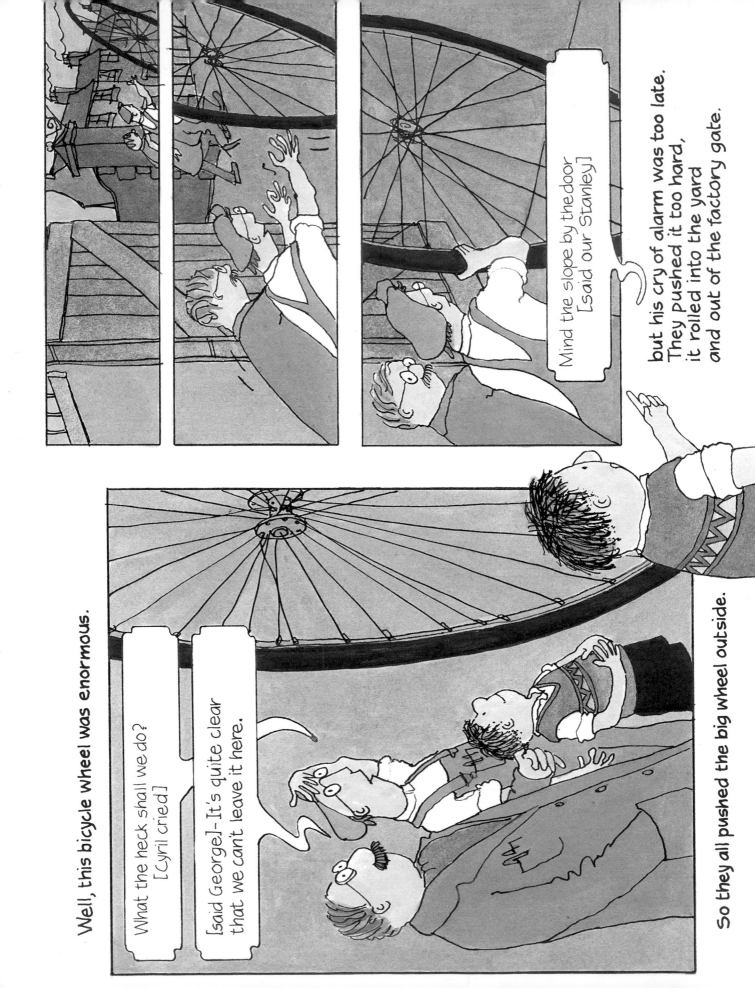

Right down the middle of Pump street it went closely followed by Cyril and Stan.

It rolled on down into Huddersgate and that's when the real fun began!

when . . . . . .

Ron Mellor was laying some concrete, and had just smoothed it out nice and flat

The runaway wheel knocked him head-over-heels, right into the concrete..............▶

It rolled on past Roebotham's cake-shop and gave Charlie Clegg such a chase.

A policeman's life is really rather dull.

He ran all through the town

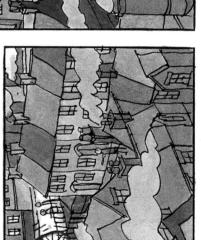

knocked a fat policeman down

and........

squashed a cream tart in his face.

The wheel rolled on through the market.

By gum! — [Cyril cried]
What a lark!

It rolled down the hill past the gasworks, and turned into Huddersgate Park.

In the park Maurice Ratcliffe was fishing, sitting there, half-asleep on his stool.

When he saw the big wheel, he let out a squeal, jumped up and fell into the pool.

[Cried Stanley]
Hey, that's not allowed!

The wheel rolled into the playground.

It rolled to the top of the playground slide, and . . . .

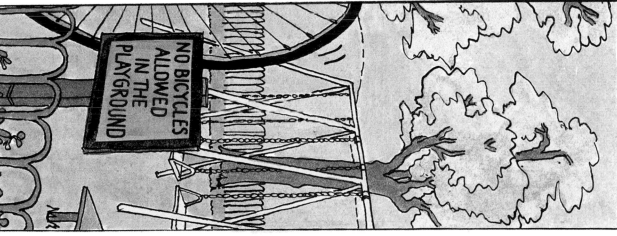

NO BICYCLES
ALLOWED
IN THE
PLAYGROUND

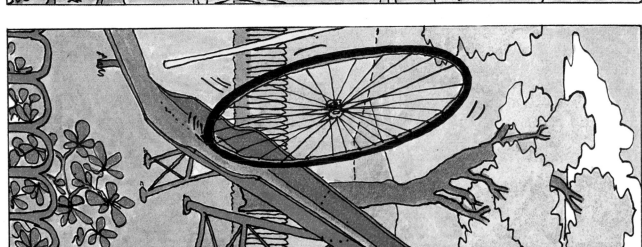

disappeared into the clouds.

Well I never.

See you.

See you Stan.

The cat caught a bird.

ROEBOTHAMS
CAKE

Doesn't complain

ROSIE'S CAFE

Alright.

And the gold-fish?

How is your Gran?

SALE

START HERE

NOT QUITE THE END

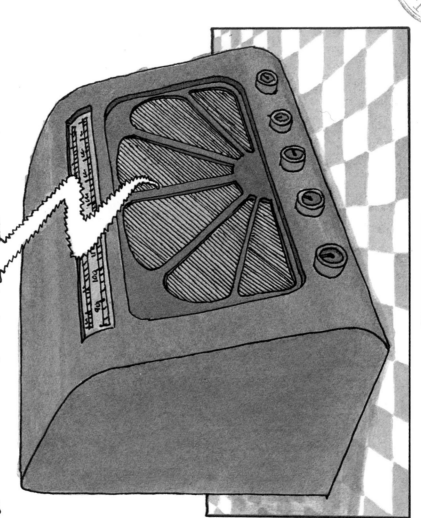